For Jo ~ N.L.
For Daniel ~ T.W.

LITTLE TIGER PRESS LTD,
an imprint of the Little Tiger Group
1 Coda Studios, 189 Munster Road, London SW6 6AW
Imported into the EEA by Penguin Random House Ireland,
Morrison Chambers, 32 Nassau Street, Dublin D02 YH68
www.littletiger.co.uk

First published in Great Britain 2010
This edition published 2017
Text copyright © Norbert Landa 2010
Illustrations copyright © Tim Warnes 2010
Visit Tim Warnes at www.timwarnes.com
Norbert Landa and Tim Warnes have asserted their rights
to be identified as the author and illustrator of this work
under the Copyright, Designs and Patents Act, 1988
A CIP catalogue record for this book
is available from the British Library

ISBN 978-1-84869-808-6
LTP/1800/4713/0322
Manufactured, printed, and
assembled in Guangdong, China.
Sixth printing, March 2022
10 9 8 7 6

The Great Monster Hunt

by
Norbert Landa

Illustrated by
Tim Warnes

LITTLE TIGER
LONDON

Early one morning, a funny noise woke up Duck.
It sounded like pShh pShh! and it came from
right under her bed.

Duck was not quite sure what it was,
and she was much too scared to look.

pShh pShh!

Instead, she jumped out of bed
and ran for help.

"Pig!" Duck yelled. "There is something under my bed, and it's making strange sounds. It goes, pshh pshh, grrr!"

"PShh pShh, **grrr**?" asked Pig. "Oh my! We need someone really strong to help. Stay right where you are!"

And Pig ran to find Bear.

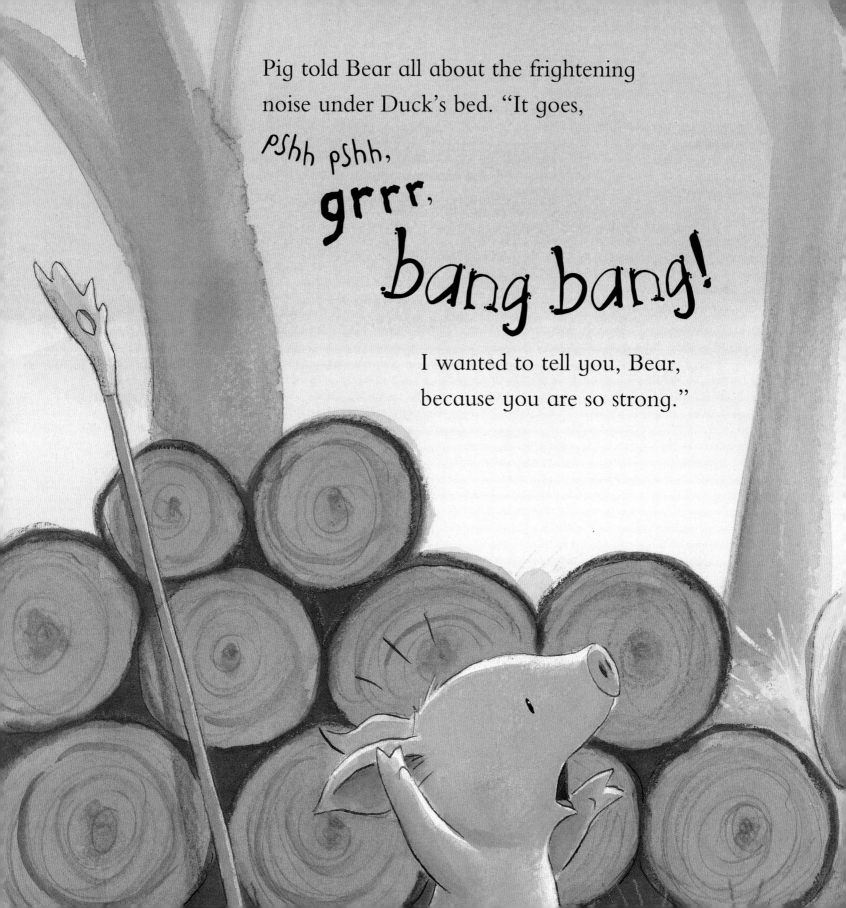

Pig told Bear all about the frightening
noise under Duck's bed. "It goes,

pshh pshh,

grrr,

bang bang!

I wanted to tell you, Bear,
because you are so strong."

Bear lifted a huge log. "It is true I am strong enough for almost anything," he said. "But I think we'd better find someone who is *loud* enough to chase this thing away."

Bear told him the dreadful news about the terrifying thing under Duck's bed.

So they ran to find Wolf, who was about to start his early morning howling.

"It goes, pshh pshh, grrr, bang bang, wham wham—

all of the time!" Bear said.

"We thought you could help us frighten it away!"

"Oh, yes, I can!" Wolf proudly said.

"There is no match for what
I can do. Just listen!

OWO oooooooo!

But maybe we also need help
from someone really clever."

So they ran to find Owl.

"Listen," Wolf said. "There is a dreadful and terrifying sound under Duck's bed. It goes, pshh pshh, grrr,

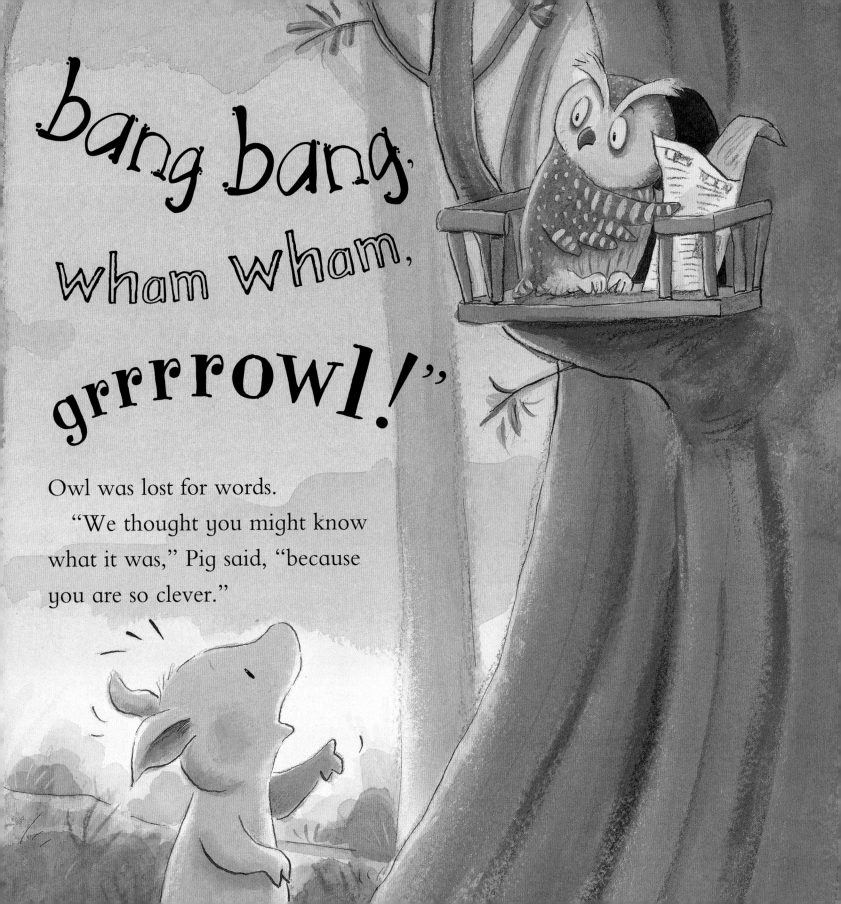

bang bang, wham wham, grrrrowl!"

Owl was lost for words.

"We thought you might know what it was," Pig said, "because you are so clever."

Owl said, "Clever, yes, that's what I am.
So I can tell you one thing:

Duck is in great danger!"

Pig, Bear, and Wolf huddled closer together.
"Are you sure?" they asked.

"Oh, yes," Owl said. "Can you imagine anything
kind and cuddly making such a noise?"

"It must be a monster!" yelled Pig.
"Oh, what are we going to do?"

"The only way to deal with
a monster," Owl said, "is to trap it."

Clever Owl!

So the animals set about gathering rope and nets and useful pokey things. Then the four of them bravely set off for Duck's house.

Owl led the way, because trapping the monster was his clever idea. Next came Wolf, howling loudly. Then came Bear, with his monster-buster stick. Last was Pig, clutching his great monster-catcher net.

Finally they arrived at Duck's house
and flattened their ears against the door.
But no monstrous sound was heard—no
screaming nor crying nor calling for help.
    "Maybe we are too late?" whispered Bear.
    "Oh, nooo!" Pig cried in despair.
    "Duck, are you there?" called Wolf.

Then the door slowly creaked open . . .

It was Duck. "You're here!" she said.
   "Duck! You are in great danger!"
whispered Bear.

"There's a monster under
your bed!" cried Pig.

Duck looked ready to faint.
"A monster?" she whimpered.
"How do you know?"

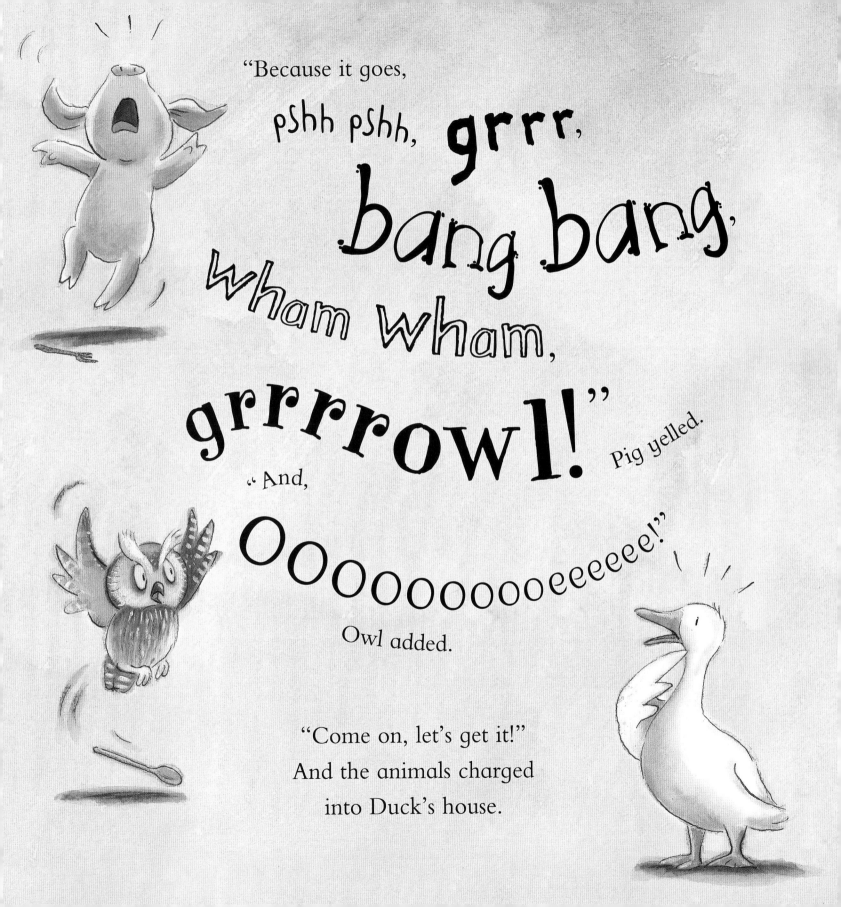

"Because it goes,

pshh pshh, **grrr**, bang bang, wham wham,

grrrrowl!" Pig yelled.

"And, OOOOOOooooeeeee!" Owl added.

"Come on, let's get it!"
And the animals charged
into Duck's house.

Up the stairs they crept . . . then they heard a sound.
    Pshh pshh! it went.
    It came from right under Duck's bed.
    Owl flashed his lantern. The animals gasped.
They could not believe their eyes!

pshh pshh!

There, right under Duck's bed, was a tiny mouse,
snoring softly in its tiny bed, pShh pShh!

"Well I never!" Duck whispered.

"Do you know what we've just done?" Owl smiled.

All feeling rather silly, the animals looked at
each other and giggled . . .

"We've just made a **monster** out of a mouse!"